Other Flossie Crums titles:

Flossie Crums and The Royal Spotty Dotty Cake
Flossie Crums and The Enchanted Cookie Tree

Flossie Crums

and the Fairies' Cupcake Ball

By Helen Nathan

Illustrated by
Daryl Stevenson

PAVILION
CHILDREN'S

To Larry xx Helen
For Ness & Ed, Amber & Chris, Maya,
Asia & Jacobi and Cass & Sass + I! Daryl x

This edition first published in the United Kingdom in 2011 by
Pavilion Children's Books
10 Southcombe Street
London W14 0RA
An imprint of Anova Books Company Ltd

Text and illustrations copyright Helen Nathan 2011
Photographs copyright Anova Books 2011
Illustrations by Daryl Stevensen

10 9 8 7 6 5 4 3 2 1

ISBN 9781843651963

Printed by 1010 Printing International Ltd, China

This book can be ordered direct from the publisher at the website: www.anovabooks.com

Have you ever wondered how fairy cakes got their name?

I used to wonder as well.

Then one day, I found out.

A note for fairy fans:

See if you can find the fairy hiding on each page. (You might have to give grown-ups a bit of help with this.)

Hello, I'm Flossie Crums!

I'm ninety-two days away from my eighth birthday, which means I'm seven and three-quarters years old.

I live at 22 Maple Syrup Lane, Little Lickington, with my brother Billie, my mum, my dad, a dog called Rocket and a cat called Goliath...

And I love baking!

My Cookery Book

by Flossie Crums

I keep all my recipes safe inside this special recipe scrapbook, and now you can share them too!

Mum

Dad

My Family

Rocket
(he's got the
swishiest tail)

Goliath
(he's so fat)

Billie (he's 6, quite annoying
and loves collecting bugs)

Did you know that every house has fairies, even yours?

Well, this is the story of how I met my fairies and discovered a fairy Kingdom, right at the bottom of my garden.

It all began one morning last summer...

I was desperate to meet a fairy, but didn't Know how. Then it came to me...

"A fairy trap!"

I shouted out loud.

"What did you say?"

asked mum as she strolled in, holding her cup of tea.

"I'm going to set a fairy trap!" I replied.
"Underneath the chestnut tree. But first I need to
bake something so amazing that even the fairies will
come out of their hiding places to have a taste. And
I know just the cake: My Very Impressive,
Especially Tasty Chocolate Cake. That should do the
trick. No one can resist that!"

But before I bake, let me show you around my kitchen and so you know what I use to bake my cakes. Then you can have a go, too.

First I need my apron and chef's hat, then a bowl, a big wooden spoon, some kitchen scales, baking tins, cupcake cases and cupcake wrappers, oven gloves and tea towels.

Now, let me show you how to make My Very Impressive, Especially Tasty Chocolate Cake.

MY VERY IMPRESSIVE, ESPECIALLY TASTY CHOCOLATE CAKE

This is the best and easiest chocolate cake recipe in the world! Even my brother Billie can make it!

My Very Impressive,
Especially Tasty Chocolate Cake

What you need:

Cake

175g/6oz/¾ cup softened butter, plus a
little extra for the cake tin
175g/6oz/¾ cup caster sugar
200g/7oz/1¾ cups drinking
chocolate powder (not cocoa)
75g/3oz/just under ¾ cup
self-raising flour
4 large eggs

Decoration

icing sugar
marshmallows or other sweets

What you do:

Ask a grown-up to preheat the oven to 190°C/375°F/gas mark 5. Use a little extra butter to grease the inside and bottom of a 20.5cm/8 inch round springform cake tin. I've used a heart-shaped tin, but round is also great!

Put all the ingredients into a large bowl and mix together with a wooden spoon until everything is really chocolaty (this will take about 3 minutes).

Scrape all the mixture into the cake tin, then get a grown-up to help put it in the oven and bake the cake for 40 minutes.

Get help to take the tin out of the oven. The cake might still be a bit wobbly in the middle when it comes out, but trust me, that's a good thing. Leave in the tin until cool.

Only when it is completely cool, gently tip the cake onto a plate and sprinkle with icing sugar. I like to decorate mine with marshmallows, but any sweets are great!

When the cake was ready I took it out to the garden with the rest of my fairy picnic. There was so much food: little sausage rolls that looked like fairy pillows, sandwiches shaped like **stars** and **heart** shaped biscuits with pink and white icing.

I laid out **acorn hats** for cups and for plates I used **seashells** I had found last time I went to the beach.

It was the **perfect** fairy trap!

How could they resist?

I hid behind the tree and waited. Fairies, I had read, are **easily frightened.**

I didn't have to wait long.

A tiny door suddenly appeared at the bottom of the chestnut tree. A beautiful fairy dressed all in pink peeked out. In her left hand she carried a lollipop wand and on her feet she wore pink slippers decorated with sweets.

I could hardly breathe. I was so excited! The fairy flitted over to the picnic, sat down and started eating the cake I had baked. **My Very Impressive, Especially Tasty Chocolate Cake!** It was unbelievable!

Then **more fairies came out of the tree**, each one wearing a different coloured dress, until there were **six little fairies** sitting on the picnic blanket, eating cake and whispering to each other.

The pink fairy then said, "This cake could be the answer to our problem. We **must** find out who baked it."

I almost **burst** with excitement!

But I didn't want to frighten them, so from my hiding place behind the tree I whispered,

"It was me."
And then I stepped out.

"I'm Flossie... Flossie Crums!"

"Oh Flossie, at last we get to meet you.

We've seen you playing in the garden f years, but we didn't know you could bal like this!" said the pink fairy. "I'm Cand and these are my friends." She pointec to the other fairies. "This is Crystal anc Cherry, Plum, Minty and that's little Honey."

Each fairy smiled at me and gave a wave.

"We're from the Kingdom of Romolonia," Candy said, pointing at the chestnut tree. "And that's our home in there."

"The Kingdom of Romolonia?" I gasped. "In our garden?"

"Romolonia is the most beautiful place," said Plum. "There are marshmallow meadows and lemonade streams and orchards of golden apples and purple pears."

"And in the winter," said little Honey, "we skate on the lemon sorbet ice rink."

"And King Saffron and Queen Rosie live in an ice cream palace that never melts," added Minty.

"Wow!" I said. "It sounds wonderful! I'd love to visit."

"Well," said Candy. "That might *be* sooner than you think. Queen Rosie has set her heart on a summer ball with beautiful cupcakes. But none of us can bake! So maybe, if you can help us make the cakes, we can get you into the Kingdom of Romolonia?"

Fairies?

A visit to Romolonia?

The chance to bake for a fairy queen?

My mind was racing. I could make mint chocolate chip cupcakes and coconut cupcakes with maple icing.

"Okay!" I shouted,
louder than I had intended.

"I'll get mum to help. We love baking together, but... oh dear! My mum will never believe I've met real fairies.

Could one of you come home wi—"

MEOW! WOOF!

Just then, **Rocket** and **Goliath** shot through the fairy picnic, scattering plates, acorn cups and My Very Impressive, Especially Tasty Chocolate Cake!

Afraid, the fairies quickly flew away through the tiny door, back home to their magical fairy kingdom.

"Oh no! You've frightened the fairies away."

I bent down and peered through the tiny door in the chestnut tree.

I could see the path that led to Romolonia, but sadly I was **far too big** to fit through the door.

The door closed with a **bang** and vanished, and my heart sank.

But then I remembered...
I had just met fairies!

I burst into the kitchen yelling for mum and Billie.
Would they believe me?

"Fairies! I knew we had fairies!

They live in the tree and they loved My Very Impressive,
Especially Tasty Chocolate Cake! Would you believe it?
And they want me to bake for the fairy ball! I'm going to
bake loads of cakes for Queen Rosie and..."

"Woah! Slow down, Flossie!" said
mum. "What do you mean fairies in
the garden? Don't talk poppicock!"

I knew she wouldn't believe me.

"But mum, I saw them.
I talked to them!"

At that very moment, something small and green fluttered out of my apron pocket and landed on the table.

It was Minty!

But before I could say a word, Billie grabbed his bug jar and slammed it down on top of the poor fairy.

"Gotchya!"

"Billie!" I screamed.

"Put your glasses on you nincompoop! She's a fairy, not a bug!"

Reluctantly, Billie let go of his catch.

"Oops, sorry," said Billie.

"I thought it was a **grasshopper!**"

Minty sat stunned for a moment. It's not everyday you get trapped in a jam jar. Then finally she found her voice and bravely said,

"Umm... excuse me Mrs Crums.
Fairies do exist.
We live in the tree, just like Flossie said, and we think Flossie's chocolate cake is the best cake in the—"

But then she stopped talking, because Mum made a funny sound and **fainted on the floor!**

After a moment, once mum recovered and was sitting comfortably on a kitchen chair, we made a list of all the cakes we needed to bake for the Fairies' Cupcake Ball.

I went to the store cupboard and got out all the ingredients I needed.

I baked and baked and the kitchen table **filled up**
with delicious plates of wonderful cupcakes.

Would you like to know how I made them?

Well, you're in luck!

I'm going to share **all** of my recipes with you.

DOUBLE CHOCOLATE CHIP CUPCAKES WITH CHOCOLATE AND PEPPERMINT CREAM ICING

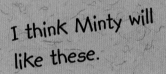

I think Minty will like these.

She loves chocolate!

Double Chocolate Chip Cupcakes with Chocolate and Peppermint Cream Icing

What you need:

Cupcakes

12 cupcake cases
115g/3¾oz/½ cup softened butter
115g/3¾oz/½ cup caster sugar
85g/generous 3oz/¾ cup self-raising flour
30g/1¼oz/¼ cup cocoa powder
2 eggs
1 tbsp milk
50g/2oz chocolate chips

Icing and decoration

a small handful of icing sugar
1 small packet of ready-to-roll white icing
¼ tsp peppermint essence
1 small packet of ready-to-roll
chocolate icing
circular biscuit cutters in different sizes
(or jam jars)
edible glue (or you could use apricot jam)
12 mint humbugs, or chocolate drops

What you do:

Ask a grown-up to preheat the oven to 190°C/375°C/gas mark 5. Put 12 paper cupcake cases into a 12-hole fairy cake tin.

Put all the cupcake ingredients into a mixing bowl and mix together for about 4 minutes until there are no lumpy bits. Spoon the mixture evenly into the cases.

Ask a grown-up to put the cake tin in the oven, then bake for 18 minutes. Once they're done, ask a grown-up to take the cupcakes out the oven and leave them to cool.

When the cakes are cool, sprinkle the icing sugar onto a clean work surface. Squeeze the white icing in your hand until it's soft, then carefully knead in the peppermint essence with your hands. Roll out the icing. To stop the icing from sticking to the worktop, wiggle the rolled icing around on the worktop and turn it each time you roll. It should be about ½ a centimeter thick.

Now roll the chocolate icing. Then use the different-sized biscuit cutters (or use different sized jam jars and something smaller, like a ketchp bottle) and cut icing circles from each colour.

Use the jam to stick one of the largest circles on top of each cupcake, then stick the rest of the circles on top of each other. Put a humbug or chocolate drop on each.

TOFFEE CANDY
AND
VANILLA CUPCAKES

Candy is the head fairy and is definitely in charge. I think she'll love these cakes with toffees on!

Toffee Candy and Vanilla Cupcakes

What you need:

Cupcakes

12 cupcake cases
115g/3¾oz/½ cup softened butter
115g/3¾oz/½ cup caster sugar
115g/3¾oz/1 cup self-raising flour
2 eggs
1 tbsp milk
½ tsp vanilla essence

Icing and decoration

400g/14oz/3¼ cups icing sugar
50g/2oz/¼ cup softened butter
2 dsp cold water
4 tbsp caramel toffee (dulce de leche)
piping bag (if you like)
12 small toffees

What you do:

Ask a grown-up to preheat the oven to 190°C/375°C/gas mark 5. Put 12 paper cupcake cases into a 12-hole fairy cake tin.

Put all the cupcake ingredients into a mixing bowl and mix together for about 4 minutes until there are no lumpy bits. Spoon the mixture evenly into the cases.

Ask a grown-up to put the cake tin in the oven, then bake for 18 minutes. Once they're done, ask a grown-up to take the cupcakes out the oven and leave them to cool.

Make the icing by slowly mixing the icing sugar with the butter, water and dulce de leche in a large bowl. After a few minutes, the icing should be gooey and glossy.

If you can use a piping bag, put the icing in the bag and pipe some on top of each cake in a big swirl or just spread the icing on with a spoon if it's too complicated! (Trust me, the cakes taste great whatever the icing looks like!)

To finish, pop a small toffee on top of each cupcake.

Black Forest Cupcake Basket with Whipped Cream and Fresh Cherries

What you need:

Cupcakes

12 cupcake cases
115g/3¾oz/½ cup softened butter
115g/3¾oz/½ cup caster sugar
85g/generous 3oz/¾ cup self-raising flour
30g/1¼oz/¼ cup cocoa powder
2 eggs
1 tbsp milk

Icing and decoration

small carton of double cream
piping bag (if you have one)
fresh cherries

What you do:

Ask a grown-up to preheat the oven to 190°C/375°C/gas mark 5. Put 12 paper cupcake cases into a 12-hole fairy cake tin.

Put all the cupcake ingredients into a mixing bowl and mix together for about 4 minutes until there are no lumpy bits. Spoon the mixture evenly into the cases.

Ask a grown-up to put the cake tin in the oven, then bake for 18 minutes. Once they're done, ask a grown-up to take the cupcakes out the oven and leave them to cool.

Make the icing by pouring the cream into a bowl and whisk until fairly stiff. If you can use a piping bag, put the cream in the bag and pipe some on top of each cooled cake in a big swirl, or just spread the cream on with a spoon if it's too complicated. Then pile high with fresh cherries!

For special occasions, once the cupcakes are cool, you can pop them into fancy cupcake wrappers which you can buy from supermarkets.

Cherry is so kind and she loves animals, even spiders (yuck!).

BLACK FOREST CUPCAKE BASKET WITH WHIPPED CREAM AND FRESH CHERRIES

Coconut Ice Cupcakes with Maple Syrup Icing

What you need:

Cupcakes

12 cupcake cases
115g/3¾oz/½ cup softened butter
115g/3¾oz/½ cup caster sugar
115g/3¾oz/1 cup self-raising flour
2 eggs
1 tbsp milk
25g/1oz/⅓ cup desiccated coconut

Icing and decoration

400g/14oz/3¼ cups icing sugar
50g/2oz/¼ cup softened butter
4 tbsp maple syrup
2 dsp cold water
piping bag (if you like)
a small saucer of desiccated coconut
12 sugar crystal 'wands'

What you do:

Ask a grown-up to preheat the oven to 190°C/375°C/gas mark 5. Put 12 paper cupcake cases into a 12-hole fairy cake tin.

Put all the cupcake ingredients into a mixing bowl and mix together for about 4 minutes until there are no lumpy bits. Spoon the mixture evenly into the cases.

Ask a grown-up to put the cake tin in the oven, then bake for 18 minutes. Then ask a grown-up to take the cupcakes out the oven and leave them to cool.

Once the cakes are cool, make the icing by mixing the icing sugar with the butter, syrup and water in a large bowl. After a few minutes, the icing should be smooth and glossy. To make the icing REALLY professional, ask a grown-up to mix the icing with an electric mixer or whisk for about 10 minutes (this is a long time, but your icing will be as fluffy and as light as a fairy!).

If you can use a piping bag, put the icing in the bag and pipe a big swirl on top of each cake, or spread the icing on with a spoon. Dip or roll your cakes very lightly in the coconut and top with a sugar 'wand'.

COCONUT ICE CUPCAKES WITH MAPLE SYRUP ICING

Crystal is so beautiful, I wanted these cakes to be really beautiful too!

Honeycomb Cupcakes with Bees

What you need:

Cupcakes

12 cupcake cases
115g/3¾oz/½ cup softened butter
115g/3¾oz/½ cup caster sugar
115g/3¾oz/1 cup self-raising flour
2 eggs
1 tbsp milk
1 tbsp runny honey

Icing and decoration

400g/14oz/3¼ cups icing sugar
50g/2oz/¼ cup softened butter
3 dsp cold water
1 tsp vanilla essence
piping bag (if you like)
4 bars of chocolate-coated honeycomb
sugar bees

What you do:

Ask a grown-up to preheat the oven to 190°C/375°C/gas mark 5. Put 12 paper cupcake cases into a 12-hole fairy cake tin.

Put all the cupcake ingredients into a mixing bowl and mix together for about 4 minutes until there are no lumpy bits. Spoon the mixture evenly into the cases.

Ask a grown-up to put the cake tin in the oven, then bake for 18 minutes. Once they're done, ask a grown-up to take the cupcakes out the oven and leave them to cool.

Once the cakes are cool, make the icing by slowly mixing the icing sugar with the butter, water and vanilla in a large bowl. After a few minutes, the icing should be smooth and glossy. To make the icing REALLY professional, ask a grown-up to mix the icing with an electric mixer or whisk for about 10 minutes (this is a long time, but your icing will be as fluffy and as light as a fairy!).

If you can use a piping bag, put the icing in the bag and pipe a big swirl on top of each cake, or spread the icing on with a spoon.

To finish, cut the honeycomb bars into chunks and pile up a few pieces on top of each cupcake. Add a few sugar bees on special occasions!

HONEYCOMB CUPCAKES
WITH BEES

These adorable little bees make these honeycomb cupcakes sweet enough even for Honey.

White Chocolate Cupcakes with Fresh Raspberry Icing

What you need:

Cupcakes

12 cupcake cases
100g/3½oz white chocolate, broken into pieces
125g/4oz/just over ½ cup butter
200g/7oz/just under 1 cup caster sugar
125ml/4fl oz/½ cup milk
1 egg
190g/6½oz/1¾ cups self-raising flour
1 tsp vanilla essence

Icing and decoration

1 packet of Renshaws raspberry-flavoured
magic melting icing (or 400g/14oz/3¼ cups
icing sugar mixed with
5 tbsp of water and
1 drop of pink food colouring)
fresh raspberries or chocolate swirls (available
in specialist cake shops)

What you do:

Ask a grown-up to preheat the oven to 190°C/375°C/gas mark 5. Put 12 paper cupcake cases into a 12-hole fairy cake tin.

Then ask the same kind grown-up to melt the chocolate in a saucepan with the butter, sugar and milk. Take off the heat and leave to cool for 10 minutes.

Scrape this mixture into a bowl and mix with the egg, flour and vanilla essence. Stir together until well mixed. Spoon the mixture evenly into the cases.

Ask a grown-up to put the cake tin into the oven, then bake for 20 minutes. Once they're done, ask a grown-up to take the cupcakes out the oven and leave them to cool.

When the cupcakes are cool, follow the instructions on the icing packet to make up the icing (or carefully mix the icing sugar, water and food colouring in a bowl) and pour onto the cupcakes. Decorate with fresh raspberries or chocolate swirls.

Plum's so clever. She loves white chocolate. I know she's going to love these!

WHITE CHOCOLATE CUPCAKES WITH FRESH RASPBERRY ICING

ROYAL ROSE CUPCAKES WITH DIAMONDS

Cupcakes fit for a queen!

Royal Rose Cupcakes with Diamonds

What you need:

Cupcakes

12 cupcake cases
115g/3¾oz/½ cup softened butter
115g/3¾oz/½ cup caster sugar
115g/3¾oz/1 cup self-raising flour
2 eggs
1 tbsp milk
½ tsp rose water

Icing and decoration

400g/14oz/3¼ cups icing sugar
50g/2oz/¼ cup softened butter
4 tbsp cold water
1 small drop of pink food colouring (if you like)
piping bag (if you like)
60 pink wafer roses
edible sugar diamonds
12 beautiful cupcake wrappers (if you like)

What you do:

Ask a grown-up to preheat the oven to 190°C/375°C/gas mark 5. Put 12 paper cupcake cases into a 12-hole fairy cake tin.

Put all the cupcake ingredients into a mixing bowl and mix together for about 4 minutes until there are no lumpy bits. Spoon the mixture evenly into the cases.

Ask a grown-up to put the tin in the oven, then bake for 18 minutes. Once they're done, ask a grown-up to take the cupcakes out the oven and leave them to cool.

Once the cakes are cool, make the icing: mix the icing sugar with the butter, water and food colouring in a large bowl. After a few minutes, the icing should be smooth and glossy. To make the icing REALLY professional, ask a grown-up to mix the icing with an electric mixer or whisk for about 10 minutes (this is a long time, but your icing gets as fluffy and as light as a fairy!).

If you can use a piping bag, put the icing in the bag and pipe a big swirl on top of each cake, or spread the icing on with a spoon.

To finish, just pop 5 wafer roses on top of each cupcake and scatter with edible diamonds! Wrap each one in a beautiful cupcake wrapper and they are ready to serve to a queen!

I was just putting the last diamond on Queen Rosie's cupcakes
when Plum and Candy flew in through the open window.

"Oh wow!" gasped Plum.

"Your cupcakes look **amazing!**

Don't they look lovely, Candy?"

"Yes!" she agreed. "And they smell incredible too.
But we need to hurry, the ball is about to begin."

I turned to mum to see if it
was okay to go to Romolonia
with my new fairy friends.

"Don't worry, Mrs. Crums," said Plum. "We'll look after Flossie and have her safely home by dark."

Mum still looked a bit worried, so I gave her a hug.

"Oh Flossie, be good," she said and kissed me on the head.

Then Plum turned to me. **"Right, Flossie, I'm going to minimize you and the cakes now. So hold tight!"** Plum waved her wand and silver stars sprayed everywhere. I felt as if I was in a tumble dryer, as the kitchen got bigger and bigger.

But it wasn't the kitchen getting **bigger**, it was me getting **smaller** and smaller!

Candy, Plum and Minty picked up the minimized cupcakes and flew out of the kitchen window and into the garden, forgetting all about me.

"Wait!" I shouted, although it sounded more like a squeak. **"What about me? I can't fly!"**

Then mum came to my rescue. She scooped me up in the palm of her hand and carefully carried me out to the tree, setting me gently on the grass.

"Have fun, Flossie," she said. "And don't forget to curtsey to the Queen!"

It was really happening!
I was about to enter the
magical Kingdom of
Romolonia for the
very first time!

Plum and Candy were talking excitedly
about the ball as we walked down the path travelling
further and further into Romolonia. I was speechless.
Everywhere I looked, there was something magical to see.

Then I saw, up on the top of a hill in the distance,
the sparkling Ice Cream Palace.

"Welcome to Romolonia, Flossie."

Minty fluttered to meet me and squeezed my hand.

"The queen can't wait to see your cakes. She's going to love them!"

Then we finally reached the Ice Cream Palace.

The palace doors were **huge** and
decorated with ice cream cones.

Plum waved her wand and the doors flew open.

It was the coolest place I have ever seen, and not just because it was made of **ice cream!**

The fairies danced about everywhere. Twirling and spinning and fluttering their wings.

Sitting majestically on their thrones sat Queen Rosie and her husband King Saffron. The Queen smiled at me and I remembered what mum had told me.

I curtsied.

I stayed at the ball for hours and learned so much about the fairies.

I found out that Minty loves my little brother, Billie. She thinks he's hilarious. Crystal is really shy and gentle, and Cherry is so kind and helpful. They all love my cupcakes so much that they now call them **fairy cakes**!

We danced and played games and drank lemonade out of the stream, but then Candy said it was time to go home.

As I was leaving, Queen Rosie smiled and presented me with a large scroll of paper, tied with a pink silk ribbon.

Once we were standing in my garden, Candy magiced me big again and I walked up to the house, feeling enormous. I unrolled the scroll. I couldn't believe it.

"Oh Flossie, you're back already. How was it darling?" asked mum.

"I've just had the best day of my life!" I grinned.

"Billie, next time you have to come too!"

I held up the paper. "Look what Queen Rosie gave me as I was leaving the ball!"

Mum gasped and Billie's eyes almost popped out of his head...

FLOSSIE CRUMS: OFFICIAL ROYAL BAKER TO THE KINGDOM OF ROMOLONIA!

Conversions

Dry Measurements

Metric	Imperial
15g	$\frac{1}{2}$ oz
30g	1oz
50g	2oz
90g	3oz
125g	4oz ($\frac{1}{4}$ lb)
150g	5oz
175g	6oz
200g	7oz
225g	8oz ($\frac{1}{2}$ lb)

Liquid Measurements

Metric	Imperial	US Cups
30ml	1fl oz	$\frac{1}{8}$ cup
60ml	2fl oz	$\frac{1}{4}$ cup
90ml	3fl oz	$\frac{3}{8}$ cup
125ml	4fl oz	$\frac{1}{2}$ cup
150ml	5fl oz	$\frac{2}{3}$ cup
175ml	6fl oz	$\frac{3}{4}$ cup
200ml	7fl oz	$\frac{7}{8}$ cup
225ml	8fl oz	1 cup
250ml	9fl oz	1 $\frac{1}{8}$ cups
300ml	10fl oz	1 $\frac{1}{4}$ cups
500ml	17 $\frac{1}{2}$ fl oz	2 cups

NB Icing sugar = confectioner's sugar;
caster sugar = superfine; self-raising
flour = self-rising flour
tsp = teaspoon
dsp = dessertspoon
tbsp = tablespoon
[The dry measurements in the conversion table differ from
ingredient to ingredient – e.g. flour and sugar aren't the same]

Here are a few helpful baking tips that
I wanted to share with you...

1. Wash your hands *before you start baking* - fairies don't like germs.
2. When making the icing, *be sure to mix really slowly at first*, otherwise the kitchen can get covered in icing sugar!
3. If the icing is too runny, you can always add a little bit more icing sugar, and if it's too stiff, just add more water.
4. Mum says it's healthier to cook with natural ingredients *because they're better for you.*
5. It's a good idea to wear an apron *so you don't get too mucky.* (Billy says he can't see the point!)
6. Always ask a grown-up to put things in and take things out of the oven for you.
7. Licking the spoon and bowl is yummy, *but it is dangerous if you have used raw eggs.* If you smile sweetly, you might *be allowed to lick the icing bowl after you have finished decorating* your fairy cakes.
8. If you enjoy cooking, always help to tidy up. My mum gets really cross if I just run off and play *before everything is clean and tidy.* (Washing up can *be quite fun really!)*

Acknowledgements

Team Flossie seems to be growing and I'd like to thank:
Polly, Becca and the team at Anova, Araminta and Philippa from LAW, Nicole from Creative Acts,
Sarah and Ruth from Renshaw Napier.
Not forgetting Kevin and Mark who have a particular love of fairies!
Special thanks to Carol, Biffy who makes me laugh and is a wonderful baker, and last but
not least the beautiful Tana!

Candy

Honey

Crystal

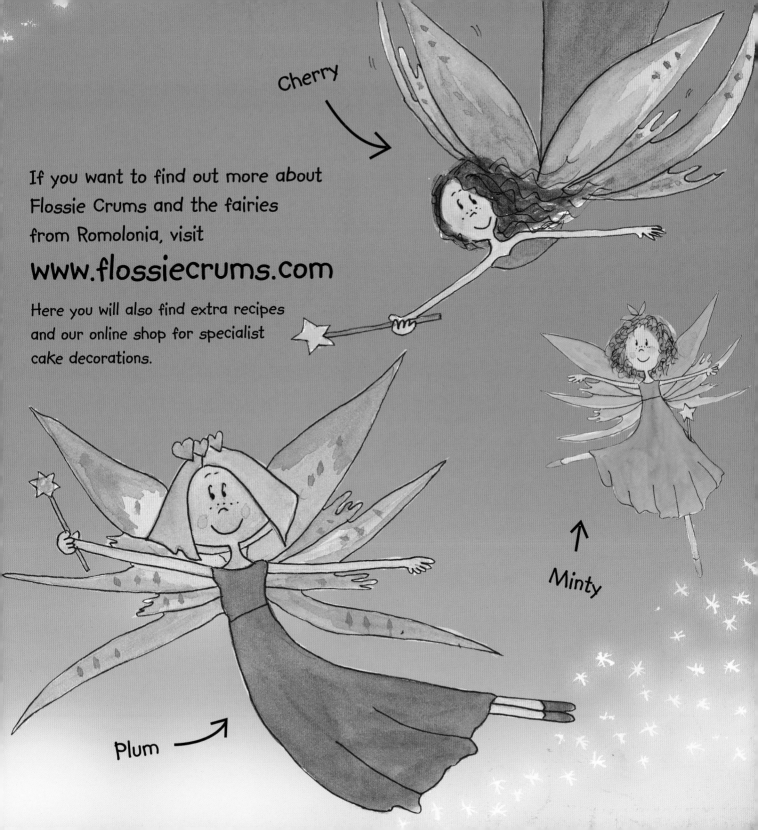

Cherry

If you want to find out more about Flossie Crums and the fairies from Romolonia, visit

www.flossiecrums.com

Here you will also find extra recipes and our online shop for specialist cake decorations.

Minty

Plum